VULNERABLE EXCELLENCE

Salvador Dalí

A view to his life's art

&

Legacy

Emiliano Martín

VULNERABLE EXCELLENCE

Salvador Dalí
A view to his life's art
&
Legacy

By Emiliano Martín

ISBN # 978-0-359-80343-9

Printed in the USA by Lulu Press, Inc.

First printing: 2019

Emiliano Martín
2955 Columbia Drive
Bensalem, PA., 19020
Poeta48@aol.com

Author's note:

Many chapters with information from this book (at the time it was a manuscript) were shared with Mike Muir, while this author was working in collaboration with him in the production of his theatrical play : "Dali- Magnificent Madness." Later, his book was published in 2018.

SYNOPSIS

"VULNERABLE EXCELLENCE " *is an original manuscript written by* **Emiliano Martín.** *It is based on the public life of Salvador Dalí, one of the greatest artists in the XX century. An interesting narration in simple terms, and informative chronological order of events, with most of the important issues that took place around the legend he created, the art he left behind, his fame and success. It is all about his deep steps in society, his dreams, his joys, and the torment of his life. Also appearing some fictional conversations that he shared with most influential people around him. Yes,* **Salvador Dalí** *was a memorable character after all.*

Dalí, without question was of one of the greatest surrealist artists of the XX century. The protagonist (Dalí) and the characters appearing through briefs episodes, sustain fictional conversations based on the author's imagination. Without getting into details the reader will enjoy knowing about moments that Dali shared with his college friends, the relationship with Gala, his wife, also his travels, people he knew and the names of artistic creations that now are still revered as icons of modern art from a man who lived his life through the character he created for himself, as an artist and a showman. Some lyrical poems were added to this production in order to bring the reader closer to the artist's provocative behavior.

The narration is easy to understand and the dialog (being fiction) brings to life all the characters by moving the reader to visualize the action taking place. One could imagine all of the scenes applicable for a play or even a movie.

With appeal to all backgrounds, young readers and people who are curious about Salvador Dali will find all the information to be very much informative, enjoyable and worth it.

INTRODUCTION:

Many things have been said and written about the one and only Salvador Dalí. Some were true and others were just fiction. Biographers all over the planet did the best they could by exposing the positive and the negative of the artist. A man of an eccentric attitude, but an exceptional mind.

Through the narration of VULNERABLE EXCELLENC - Salvador Dalí, we will find an honest attempt to establish in chronological order, most public knowledge events in the life and art of one of the greatest surrealist in the XX century.

The narration is based on a series of stories made public from the media. Over the years, articles have appeared in newspapers, magazines, radio and TV interviews, even word to mouth information or rumors if not gossip that somehow became available through social conversations all over the world. Therefore this narration is no more than an interpretation of all of the above.

The dialogs are fiction and the poems are just thoughts with a personal touch from its author, who believes that "any resemblance with reality is pure coincidence."

Index   Page

WHO IS WHO... THROUGHOUT THE NARRATION

Due to the long and productive life of Salvador Dalí it is almost impossible to recount the exact number of his associates, acquaintances, enemies and friends, who for whatever the reason is, at one time or another, became an influence in the diverse existence and achievements of one of the greatest artist in the world, if not the greatest in the surrealist art.

Just a handful of people are mentioned below :

Narrator : *the voice who simply tries to add the author's dramatic personal interpretation of most of the well known facts and rumors about the life of the artist.*

Salvador Dali: is the controversial artist who became a legend in his own time.

Salvador Dalí i Cusi... father of Dalí and a lawyer by profession, very strict individual of high morals. At first was supportive of his son's artistic interest. Later on in life things changed.

Felipa Domenech Ferrés... mother of Dalí and supportive of her son. She died young.

Ana Maria Dalí is the sister of the painter and very close to her brother. She became a model forthe early days of the artist and forever grateful to him.

Elena Ivanovna Diakonova (Gala) is a Russian born and married woman who visits Spain and meets **Dali** in his home town to become his muse. After a friendly divorce with her French husband, she stayed with **Dalí** for fifty years; marrying him in a civil ceremony. Years later she married the painter again in the catholic church. The weddings also took place in Spain.

Paul Eluard is the French surrealist poet and the first husband of **Elena Ivanovna Diakonova.** Later known universally as **Gala.** This name was given to her by Dalí, her new husband.

Cécile Éluard is the daughter of **Gala** and Paul **Eluard. B**orn in France and raised by her father with no much contact with her mother, she lived to be 99 years old.

Ramón Pichót, is a reputable local painter and friend of the Dalí's family. A very influential individual in Dalí's passion for painting.

André Breton is the French poet and literary critic besides being the leader of his surrealist movement. He thought of the presence of **Dalis** as despicable.

Max Ernst is a German artist, poet and painter as well as a pioneer of the DADA movement. He shared part of his life with Gala and Paul Eluard in a "ménage a trois" situation. He knew about Dalí, but never met him in person.

Sigmund Freud is a neurologist by profession, acclaimed by his peers and founder of psychoanalysis dialog between doctor and patient.

José (Pepin) Bello is a medical student with living quarters at the Residence of students of Madrid. He is the first person to meet and welcome **Dali** upon his arrival in Madrid. He also knew other students that would be introduced to Dali and soon they all became a group of friends with common artistic interest. He lived to be 103 years old and made it to see the XX century.

Luis Buñuel is an agriculture student also living in the Residence where he is introduced to **Dali** becoming good friends with him. As a movie's director he achieved international fame and allowed Salvador Dali to collaborate in his early movies.

Federico Garcia Lorca is a law student in Madrid and part of the group. He kept a special relationship with **Dali** and the two of them shared their artistic juices with mutual admiration.

Rafael Alberti is another friend of the group although he was not a student in residence like the rest of the group mostly run by **José (Pepin) Bello**. He also painted and wrote poetry becoming a literary icon of fame in the Spanish poetry world.

Ignacio Sanchez Mejias is a bullfighter and an admirer of the arts, yet being a close friend of José (Pepin) Bello, he soon joins the group of artists who seem to be going places.

Argentinita is a Flamenco dancer and not a student in Madrid like the rest of the group, but being a close friend of Ignacio Sánchez Mejias and José (Pepin) Bello she could not help the temptation of being part of the group of students/friends... always run by the energy of José Bello, better known as Pepín.

Professor/ Dean of the School is a fictional character based on the event that happened in the Academy of Fine Arts in Madrid and the story behind Dalí's expulsion from school.

AN ARTIST OF MANY FACES

Narrator :

The name "Salvador Dalí" is a recognizable emblem associated with the school of surrealism, although the painter, could pacify any humor; any school of art including the classics, or even cubism. And yet it is surrealism that was taken to another level with his talent and imagination, brushes and colors over oil canvas at his command.

The man with his personal behavior and the artist that he was, were antagonizing forces 180 degrees apart. With his mind always in gear, thinking or perhaps dreaming of the next step forward, he became a complete artist with an insatiable instinct to define the things to come.

Author of near fifteen thousand works of art... he somehow decided that it was not enough.

He went to work in the movies providing ideas not just for the story or the script, but counseling on decorations for background scenes and wardrobe.

As a poet, Dalí wrote interesting thoughts and in prose he published his own biography, not realizing that he still had forty more years to go on.

Being a good draftsman, Dalí was able to sculpture fine objects and human figures. Either on wood, clay or bronze... all became banners of his art.

His designs with jewelry soon caught up with high society; with furniture and selected home appliances, he raised the eyes of people who could not believe the trend of this new ideas; the result of his crazy genius and craft.

Also a designer of clothes he placed his name as a trademark. The "Dalí shirt" as he announced on Spanish TV, became a fashionable and popular product, and he kept going on to add his imagination to architectural engineers when designing a big castle for his wife. With all this around him, his paintings did not fall behind. Salvador Dalí remained as much admired as criticized worldwide. His magnificence was moved between pure madness and a genius from within not knowing when to give up.

Considering that at age thirty he is a financially broke individual with no much future in front of him, but the challenge, struggle and perseverance in order to intrude in a well established world of fine artists all over the world.

Without question Salvador Dalí had an attractive life and at the same time... life made him rich and famous, an artist larger than life. Amazingly so, it took less than twenty years for him to be found on top of his artistic achievements, not only financially, but having completed works of art very much adored by all who saw him coming as a true messiah in the surrealist frame of art. Dalí never tried to slow down, he moved like a "globe trotter" amazing the crowds who visited his painting exhibits and responded so vividly.

His behavior in public, viewed as extravagant and ridiculous, satirical with the clout of a can man or a genius from out of space. Pure madness from an artist like no other a true divine craziness not seen before in an artist of that magnitude.

1904 - SALVADOR DALI IS BORN FOR THE SECOND TIME

Narrator:

The Dalí family, financially settled and comfortably leaving in Cadaques, were expecting the arrival of the first child. He was a healthy looking boy who brought joy and pride for all around him. He was named Salvador.

Life, with a surprise of its own, unmercifully put an early fatal dent in the childhood of Salvador. Followed by a sudden death both parents were devastated while attending a Christian funeral for the young boy. Time went on and the couple were blessed with the announcement of a new addition to the family. This child to be, was very much wanted and expected to be another boy. Once he was born, the baby was baptized with the name of Salvador, like the deceased brother. This time the new Salvador would grow up to become more than the replacement of the brother he never new.

Dalí:

I will be forever grateful to live with my brother's soul, to feel his limitless notion of being alive in me. I often find being caught between heaven and the earth, between dreams and real life, between fantasy thoughts and the facts of our lives. Yet my brother is with me.

Since I was a little child, my father has always told me, that I was purely conceived to carry on the life of my lost brother, the one I have never known since I was not even born at the time of his death, but at the same time I feel him standing around me, alone, and guiding and exercising his will in me. My father always kept saying that I was the reincarnation of my brother Salvador, and I believe him on behave of the two of us.

Narrator:

Young Salvador Dalí was a normal child, kind and studious, and very much adept to learning drafting and color painting. Growing up, Dalí was always influenced by his father whose ideas about life, superstition and religion had a negative form of education in the life of the great artist to be.

His mother, on the contrary, she was much supportive of her son who at the same time revered her with devotion.

1914- YOUNG DALI AT THE BEACH

Narrator :

He definitely was a well behave child, very observant and willing to learn in school. While at the same time he played street/beach soccer with friends, he always demonstrated a passion for the arts. Young Salvador Dalí was always two steps ahead of the rest of the pack, avid in his thinking, his keen ability for the creation of new drawings, soon emerged bringing people's attention.

While attending high school in 1916, he was able to proudly present and enjoy his own and first art exhibit. Dalí felt in heaven and enthusiastically driven by good comments from his peers, teachers and the small town neighbors at large.

His mother become the propeller in high gear to provide him good support. Through the entire summer time, the family spent days in the quiet Mediterranean beach town of Cadaques.

There, young Dalí took notes and sketched everything appearing in front of his eyes, the Mediterranean beach, the waves, the sky, the sun and the moon were subjects he could practice with desire and technique. He was at peace with himself.

When using the oil canvas and colors, he added a touch of artistic beauty already immersed in the style of the young artist. His sister Maria, become his constant admirer and a model for his early paintings. It was a unique relationship between brother and sister transforming young Dalí into the famous painter he eventually would become.

1915- YOUNG DALI AND RAMON PICHOT

Narrator:
The town of Cadaques and its tranquil beach were the perfect place where the Dali family would spend the summer months to relax. Away from the fuss of the big city like Barcelona it was a heaven where nothing appeared to happen, except for a local fishing crew pursuing their daily business. At the same time, a handful of artists made their presence looking for peace of mind and inspiration.

Ramón Pichót, a friend of the Dalí's family, an honest man with a solid reputation as a local painter who used to spend quality time at the beach was a familiar face.

Pichót :
Hello Salvador! It is good to see you again. So you and your family are back for vacation?

Dalí :
Yes Sir. Thank you for asking. We just came two day ago and here we are, one more time and ready to spend quality time once more. Besides, summer is always fun. I am ready.
This time I brought all my painting tools and I plan to used them as soon as we get set around the house.

Pichót :
Yes, I hear you are still working with your drawings and doing a good job in school. You keep at it and try to learn as much as you can. There is a lot of talent out there but if you are good you will surpass everyone and maybe show up as a leader. Just remember never to give up.

Dalí :
Thank you Mr. Pichót, I also admire your work. I always try to take a pick at the kind of work you do. Although I admit, personally I am

attracted by the classics; I try to study and practice their techniques, but please, Mr. Pichót, allow me a question. In your honest opinion, if you do not mind... what is the artistic school of your choice ? or where do you feel more comfortable with...?

Pichót :

Well, I do not mind the question, and I am glad you asked. The classics are and always will be the ones to learn from. As to what school is better... There is not an easy answer. When you paint for pleasure, you decide what is better for you. If you paint for money, it is different. The public's taste it is what moves the direction of the market. Obviously the school of Impressionism is doing well right now, but recently there is a move towards the non conforming ideas with structure of its own, perhaps no structure at all.

All the new French poets are good at it with poetic words, and it surely works; they call it "Surrealism." The painters too want to give it a try with a vision and images of individual interpretations for anything appearing to be abnormal, illogical, and not real, at least for the conservative minds, who in my opinion still leave in the past. But it is early to know for sure. We shall see to that.

Dalí :

Mr. Pichót. That sounds interesting "abnormal and illogical and not real." That sounds interesting and I like the idea as much as it is new to me. Please, tell me more about that school of surrealism. I want to know..

Pichót :

Let me tell you Salvador, once you see it, there is an abundance of energy emerging from the colors, angles and shapes, even the absurd blends with the intelligence of someone's dreams and ideas. There is a visual contact with magic to bring life to new and old, to reason with the unconscious to replenish any soul.

Dalí :

Mr. Pichót, I think I could become addicted to that sort of thing. I can feel its magnetism. You know? I often close my eyes and get lost within the scheme of shadows and lights taking me to a newly deformed set of objects, humans and animals like floating in space. Have you ever experienced or tried to paint something like that?

Pichót :

Sure…! I have a couple of paintings of that nature, but I am afraid I am getting old to get involved with new tricks. Yes Salvador, nothing new is ever easy, yet you could fall for it. I had traveled to Paris on several occasions and witnessed the artistic scene of fashionable styles, igniting the passion of young artist. Actually, I was impressed and pleased with "surrealism."

Since then I became truly convinced that what I saw there, it was the style to be in and I still believe it. Paris, is an oasis of artists of all tastes. Any artist must go there. And you must be there to experience it someday. Soon, God willing and with the approval of your parents.

Dalí :

Mr. Pichót, I surely am enjoying this conversation, I am learning from you and I would love to acquired some of the techniques you have mentioned. Now I am excited about it as much as I am proud of you.

Narrator : *Dalí was observant and listened to Pichót, while carefully learning some tricks in the craft, becoming fully aware that the first chance at hand, he would gladly go to Paris and see for himself the promised land, the place where surrealism was taking off to fly way up high.*

Pichót, could not help it, but almost unconsciously he was definitely setting up a solid foundation in the young Dalí's.

The thrill for painting with a surrealist imagination became a deep obsession for young Dalí and an asset for both painters. Together they continued sharing thoughts, colors and canvases at the Mediterranean beach.

1916- SALVADOR DALI AND HIS MOTHER FELIPA

Narrator :
The relationship between mother and son was always a solid one, while at the same time the small town of Figueras was the perfect place to live for the Dalí's family.

Felipa :
Salvador, my child, you behave nicely at home and school.... I am so proud of you.

Dalí :
Thank you mother, I love you too.

Felipa :
Your father and I are very pleased with the way you handle things. It is a joy to watch you growing up as the nice young man you are.

Your sister Ana Maria is also a fan of yours. With a family like this we are indeed blessed by God. In a way it is a shame to think that someday, we all may have to move on forward; perhaps in different ways, but that is life.

Dalí :
Mother, I know you are the best mother on Earth and I would not be here if it was not because of you. You and father are good providers and my sister and I feel fortunate to be your children. I count my blessings and pride, thanks to you all.

Narrator :
Young Dalí was avidly learning from people around him. He was a true observant of nature, and yet he could easily get lost in his own ideas, wandering alone in space. His mind could work intensely making him to behave like a tenacious dreamer.

Felipa :

Salvador, I have been in your school chatting with the director, he just gave me some good news. You are doing well, the teachers are happy with you and you must maintain your positive behavior. Besides, they advice for you to keep up with your drafting/painting practices to learn as much as you can. Your teacher will make a firm recommendation for you for enroll in the best school in Madrid.

Dalí :

Madrid…? That is a big far away place mother, we are Catalans and happily living in a small town like this. We have family and friends, we love it here. We do not know anyone in Madrid. Frankly, if I have to make a long trip like that, I would rather go to Paris. There is where the artists go. Specially the new surrealist.

Felipa :

Well, my son, Paris is a foreign land. For that experience you need maturity, besides improving your French. Right now your father agrees with me. At the same time Madrid is not far by train and there are many young students from all over Spain. I am sure that Madrid will do you good. First get a good education and later on, travel and see the world, if that is what you wish. I know you will conquer whatever you so desire.

Dalí :

Mother, I do appreciate your words, I always liked our town and the thought of being away makes me think how much I will miss you and father. I will miss Ana Maria, my dearest sister. Let me tell you mother, at times she has been modeling for me and she is really doing a good job. I am proud of her too. She is a good sister. And you are my lovely and dear mother.

Felipa : I am happy to hear that. Well, Salvador, let us take one day at the time. First finish school here, in our town and in the days to come… God will help us to decide.

Narrator :

And so it was that Dalí was heading to one of the most prestigious schools in Spain. Before it happened in 1921, Dalí's mother died of breast cancer. The young man was only 16 years old.

He always said that his mother's death was the greatest blow he could have experienced in life. Salvador Dalí made the trip to Madrid, the capital of Spain and he was enrolled into the "Real Academia de Bellas Artes de San Fernando." From that time on, his life would turn into something new and totally unexpected that would mark forever, not only his character but his existence as an artist on Earth.

Almost simultaneously Dalí's father married again, this time took for espouse the sister of his deceased wife.

There was an acceptance by young Dalí and the rest of the family. He never showed a sense of resentment for the marriage of his aunt.

1922- PEPIN MEETS DALI IN MADRID (LUCK OR COINCIDENCE)

I was heading out and almost pressed for time
I ran down the steps to the lobby.

There, while crossing the hall, I saw at the entrance door
someone with looks of a new student who appeared to
be lost upon his arrival to the "Students Residence" of
Madrid.

Two suitcases were his luggage. Besides his provincial
clothes, he offered an image of secrecy, mysteriously
attractive for a young man of few words.

I couldn't help being supportive when he asked for
directions to reach the second floor. ***"Thank you....!
I am Salvador Dali."*** He quickly responded with a non
Castilian accent. His voice was firm and strong.
I told him that he was welcome and that around here, I
was known simply as Pepín.

It took no more than two days for us to become good
friends. With Dali, conversation was not easy for he kept
things to himself, yet if pushed against the corner, he
could erupt in contempt with no fear of authority but a
degree of intelligence in a tone of a surrealist sarcasm I
have not witnessed before.

He told me he was a painter and interested in poetry,
That was good news to me, since I had already met
a small group of individuals with the same affinity.

They all were young men destined to be among the
greatest names in the XX century.

The great Federico García Lorca, the filmmaker Luis Buñuel
and the distinguished poet Rafael Alberti.
There were the embers of a camaraderie and friendship
that I was able to share, daily. Let us call it luck or coincidence,
but together, we built memories and now… the rest is history.

*Narrator: José Bello (Pepín), college student in Madrid, soon began
to make friends with Dali and Lorca with whom he shared the same
room at the Student's Residence in Madrid. Being also a good friend
of Rafael Alberti and Luis Buñuel, he acted on behave of the group by
organizing readings and exhibits among other students.*

*Pepín, (little Joey) as he was known by his friends, together with his
cultural brother and pal Ignacio Sánchez Mejias came up with the
idea of organizing a gathering of poets and writers to celebrate the
CCC anniversary of the death of Luis de Gongora.*

*Pepín and Ignacio, personally wrote letters and invitations to
everyone available to assist the meeting in Cordoba (Spain). Most
literary figures in Spain attended. The year was 1927 and the event,
with its gathering of poets and writers became a historical success
for what the rest of the country and even the world in literary terms,
has known as "the generation of 1927."*

*Pepín outlived all his college friends and died having well over past
his 100 birthday.*

1922- DIALOG AMONG STUDENTS WHILE IN COLLEGE IN MADRID

Narrator :

As college students this group of friends (Alberti, Lorca, Dalí, Buñuel and Pepín) meet, and make plans to go out together in the evening, while at the "Students Residence" of Madrid.

Alberti :

I am pleased to meet you Salvador, and welcome to Madrid.

Dalí :

Thank you... That is kind of you.

Alberti :

So I hear that you are another painter and a writer....
One more for the competition, I guess. At least our friend PEPIN uses his imagination to gather girls in Madrid. Oops...! Sorry Federico, we know that you only love poetry.

Lorca:

That's true.... I feel an ejaculation when I read and use my pen, when I'm totally free and able to smear on paper any thought in verse or prose, when I face the circumstances making me feel no remorse.

Dalí :

That's well said from any fine poet who writes and can love with passion as long as the lyrics flow while propelled by the enthusiasm of the heart and the inner soul. And yet we could also say that writing becomes a chance to show off.

Alberti :

Oh yes. Salvador Dalí. I really don't believe this.

You can also speak in verse. I was told you were an artist of enormous qualities with the brushes and the canvas and perhaps some melody behind colors for the abstract touching the line of the obscene. Sorry friends… no offense to anyone!

Pepín :

C'mon guys… will you stop putting aside petty comments
taking us to nowhere land. Besides, now that we know one another
let's get ready, time is up to go out to center city and together have some fun.

I've heard that Ignacio Sánchez will bring his "Argentinita." Let me tell you: she can dance…!

Alberti :

She can surely dance, Ignacio enjoys the bullring, Salvador can paint, we can write and read poetry, and you Señor Buñuel can talk and direct the orchestra.

Oh yes, together we can do it all. What a gang…!
Well Pepín? with so much talent you could soon organize a gathering of performing artists.

I know you like that sort of thing. That is why we all love you.

Buñuel :

Oh c'mon people. This is enough. I have been waiting downstairs for over fifteen minutes and there is no time to waste. The evening is young, but hurry up you all. Keep moving right now…!

Alberti :

Yes let's go…! We do not want to disappoint to anyone. Saturday night is waiting for us to enjoy it all we can.

Dalí :

That sounds like a commitment on behave of the group. I am on board.

Narrator :
Soon they all became good friends and together were able to share the memory of unforgettable moments in their college years in Madrid.

1923- PRIVATE DIALOG BETWEEN LORCA AND DALI

Narrator :
Federico García Lorca with Salvador Dalí while at the "Students Residence" in Madrid, circa 1923.

Lorca :
I am so glad that you are here.
I keep looking to your paintings and I remain magnetized,
feeling the juices of enthusiasm running through my veins.
Salvador, you inspire me, I feel better knowing you.

Dalí :
Federico, I do truly enjoy your company.
You are kind and your compassion makes my juices flow at ease.
When you read I feel in heaven, but thirsty for poetry;
I need more coming from you.
You are like flames from a fire which warmth I cannot resist.

Lorca :
Oh Salvador, your sensual and charming personality
sinks at anything you aim.
Having an effect on me I would love to be the canvas
while you color over me with the skill
of a master like you, breaking barriers to be free.

Dalí : You are really a handsome man with sparkles of emotion
filling in my fantasy.
And the stream of flowing verses that you could write over me
I shall carry on forever deep in my heart that believes
that you are not just a poet, but someone who can achieve
a name for eternity.

1922-1926 MADRID - ACADEMIA DE BELLAS ARTES
(Academy of Fine Arts)

Narrator :

By 1922, the year when Salvador Dalí attended the prestigious "Academia de Bellas Artes de San Fernando" in Madrid, he made many friends who believed in his ability as a fine artist. Some art exhibits among the students were set up in the school's hallways and Dali showed up as an idol for his supporters. Soon he would find that his demeanor in the pursuit of excellence would be vulnerable.

It only took one solid year for Dali to have one more encounter in school with the powers that be.

Dalí :

I am here to support the chair of the painting school on behave of a fellow student who I admire and very much deserves to be appointed to such position.

Dean of the school :

Mr. Dalí, I admire your courageous decision, but that call is not up to you, but the board of professors and acting judges from the school. This institution has rules, a system and a traditions we must preserve. You should understand that!

Dalí :

Sir, this is important for the students. The least you can do is to allow the students to join the judges. It is not fair that students have no voice within these walls.

Dean of the school :

You are one of our many students. You are here only to learn and you have no right to come to my office to tell me how to handle my business for the school.

Dalí :

Oh yes Sir, I believe to have a right to express my opinion. You see, my father is paying for you to have a job here, while you take a seat behind your desk. And frankly, we the students need our voice to be heard.

Dean of the school :

I will pretend that I heard no words from your mouth. This conversation did not exist and no student will use that tone of voice with me. You may step out my office. Right now!

Dalí :

Sir, I will leave the office because you asked me to do so, but I will share this issue with my fellow students and make sure that I protest the mediocre way of thinking by you, and others like you in the school.

Narrator :

The choice of words made in public to protest the judge's motion was costly and Dalí was on his way out and forced to repeat the scholastic year under the threat of expulsion.

Time went on and back home, by 1924 he placed his first commercial publication with illustrations for a book of poetry titled "Els bruixes de Liers." ("The witches of Liers.")

The book was written in the Catalan dialect by his childhood friend Carles Fages, now an emerging author and poet. Not much fuss came from the book, but the illustrations from Dalí had not only a quick acceptance but a curious tone of interesting and special appeal. At last Dalí rejoined the Academy of fine Arts only to get in trouble again with the School Tribunal evaluating his works.

Professor :

Sr. Dalí, this is an exam and I do not approve your work, it needs to be improved. I shall give you one more chance to touch it up or come up with a better version.

Dalí :

A better version of my painting? This, I offer to you, Sir, It is art at its best. Something original and fruit of my imagination. It is entirely mine and I am proud of it, Sir, think about what you have said about my presentation.

Professor :

I do not have to think about anything. And you simply need to do a better job, by using a real technique and appropriate colors for the subject you paint. I am telling you as a teacher of art. You ought to listen for once.

Dalí :

You, a teacher of art...? It may be so, but... **"I am a genius."** You certainly have admitted that you do not understand my art. As you can see, we both are at different levels of art's perception. And I will not compromise.

Narrator :

Something had to be done with that sense of narcissism and rude behavior. The school decided to expel Salvador Dalí for life from the Academy. His rebellious words were not going to be tolerated.

Today, part of that institution is a fine museum of art. The name Salvador Dalí is not listed among the graduates, however some time ago and facing the unequivocal success of the painter, as a gesture of acknowledgment before history, he received just a "student mention of attendance" at the Academia de Bellas Artes in Madrid.

The incident of Dalí's expulsion from school was meant to be a lesson for the student, or save face for the Academy, Dalí did not care much. He left Madrid and went home with the energy and ambition to fulfill all of his dreams. In other words, from that moment, "Dalí, the character" was born and ready to go.

Nevertheless and before he started his self promotion career as an artist, he was called to arms and served his country in uniform at the end of 1926. The new dictator in Spain, general Primo de Rivera had recently taken over the power in government and had called to arms all young men in the country, including the sons of rich families who up to that time could pay money to someone else for taking over the place of the rich kid. Even so, thanks to the family influence, Salvador Dali, the soldier, was sent to the castle of San Fernando, an old fortress and military camp very close to his home town. In that place is where the out of school man, fulfilled his military duties in the army of Spain for only nine months. That short amount of time in the service was unheard of in those days.

While Salvador Dalí was able to enjoy his privilege (whatever it was...) At that time, other young men of his age, had to serve the compulsory service to the nation, in uniform, in the cruel and prolonged Spanish–Moroccan war, fought over the Spanish colonies in the North African territory.

1929- PAUL ELUARD BREAKS UP WITH GALA OVER SALVADOR DALI

Narrator : It has been a while since the wonderful summer days when the arrival of the married couple took place in the beaches of Costa Brava, north of Barcelona in the northeast corner of Spain. It was an increasingly enjoyable good time, especially for the wife (Elena Ivanovna Diakanova) who contemplates the idea of staying a bit longer due to having made the acquaintance of the young painter Salvador Dalí. Especially since she takes all the attention provided by the artist, who at the same time asks her to model for him. Loving that degree of attention she is having the time of her life.

On the other side, her husband, Paul Eluard is not showing signs of excitement. He simply wanted to go back home, to France.

Eluard :
Don't you think it is the right time to go back home. We have met Dalí, we have seen the place and this is no longer the nice weather we knew when we first came, besides I do miss Paris, its ambient, and my native French.

Gala :
I am not sure what you mean. We seem to have all we need. This is tranquil and seductive and not an expensive place to live either. Besides, we are by the sea with its fresh air and most of the time, a blanket of blue sky is above us, also the local food and people with its culture. This is a charming and a cute inspiring little town. You are a poet. You should know and understand that.

Eluard :
Cute and Charming? Perhaps! Inspiring? I would call it interesting. Culture. There is not much culture here, unless you refer to the painter you seem to be so fond of. At first I thought he would be different from others and intriguing. Now he is using you as a model.

So much for a surrealist painter. And believe me… I know that you are a lover of surrealist art. Now you are acting like a lover of a surrealist painter. Frankly I am not sure of what you are.

Gala :
Paul, be patient and listen to me, please. What I am is not important. Yet, I've always known the importance of what I want. Seriously, right now I like the feeling of being closer to the paintings of Dalí. The feeling is great. And that matters to me.

Eluard :
=Don't be ridiculous. I don't wish to hear that, you are falling for that creepy surrealist fellow, he makes me wonder sometimes. He often acts like an immature human, besides he must be at least ten years younger than you.

Gala : And so what…?
I am not old… I am very much alive. And to be exact my dear Paul, in all the years I have shared with you, right now I am excited more than ever, and for other reasons. Yes it is like something new. And Salvador makes me feel alive, much more than I used to feel in the past.

Eluard :
Oh no…! that is why you hang around him with such vigor, I know that he calls you "Gala." And you like that. I never thought this whole thing could lead up to this point. Frankly: if that is how you feel, I am glad for you, but I do not get it nor do I want to understand it. I am just tired of this ridiculous if not sad situation.

Gala :
Well now…! You never complained when I shared you with the great **Max Ernst**. We had a nice "ménage á trois." Remember that? Oh you seem to have forgotten already… So don't you tell me now about your feelings… like "being tired of this or that" or anything else… for that matter. Please, accept it. I have already told you that right now, I feel very much complete with Salvador. He is relaxing to be with and excitable to me.

Eluard : My dear, we have a young daughter waiting for our return. With or without feelings… we cannot be here forever. Cecile needs an education and this is not our home. As matter of fact we are in a foreign land.

We both know that we do not belong here and we do not have to make a big deal out it. We can easily go back and take this vacation as an experience.

Gala :

My darling, I left my home a long time ago. I simply make my home as I move along, you know that by now. As far as our daughter Cecile, you are best suited for her. Anyway I never saw myself in the role of being a good mother, perhaps not even just a mother. On the contrary you have always been a fine father to her.

Eluard :

Oh, c'mon Gala, you cannot be serious. Are you saying this is over…? This is final between us…? Well, if this is the way you want it, there is no more to do here. You win, at least for now, as for me I had enough. I shall return to or daughter and I wish you well in the future.

Narrator :
Soon after this situation, Paul Eluard returned home, to France and maintained an amiable divorce with Gala. She remained in Spain and lived with Dalí in a small cottage off the north coast of Barcelona. A couple of years later, still in Spain, they were married in a civil ceremony. That was in 1934

1931- SALVADOR DALI AND HIS SISTER

Narrator :

The relationship between Dalí and Gala is in full gear. This is not accepted by his father, who angrily disapproved his son's behavior, not only as family business but denouncing it in public. Things got to be bad to the point that the artist is out of the family will. Dali and Gala, independently live together in a nearby seacoast town while doing their own thing. They, as a couple, do not care much about family or other's opinion.

Dalí :

Yes Ana, so nice of you to drop by, please come in. My dear sister, you are always welcome here.

Ana María :

Thank you Salvador, you look great. Oh my sweet brother, we do not live too far apart
from each other, but I miss you so much. Actually we all do… but where is Gala?

Dalí :

Sorry you missed her. She just went out to the beach. Looking for a tan under the sun, she always enjoys the waves and the wind. She will be back shortly.

Ana María :

I understand Salvador. Judging from all the new paintings I can tell you have been busy and I am happy for you and the devotion you manifest for the craft you are so good at. I miss my modeling sessions for you, but I know that life has to go on. Definitely, I do not want to be nostalgic, but I am your sister and I would like to be near you, I need to know more about your new ideas, the work you are involved with and whatever you want to share with me.

Dalí :

Well, Ana, I still do not understand father. I know that when mother died it was a big vacuum in his life. We all felt that way, but we are adults and we must have our own   lives. Right now he keeps reproaching my moves like if I were a delinquent person. I never said one word when he married mother's sister. Our own aunt. And yet, since I got involved with Gala, he told me to get lost and away from home. He must think I am sick, that Gala and I are like a contagious dieses.

Ana María :

Please do not feel that way. Do not be sad. Father is the way he is and his new wife, our aunt, is a decent human being. She has nothing but love for us. We are still a family and I need you to understand that.

Dalí :

Yes, but in the meantime I am out of the family's house and father's will, I am on my own with Gala and struggling to sell my paintings. I am not angry, I am hurt, but that is all right. I know that someday I will show you all what the genius that I am is capable of . Yes, Salvador Dalí, and that is me, the one who will never surrender to no one. Someday I shall prove to the world that I am an artist like no other have existed on Earth.

Ana María :

That is my brother. The one and only artist I truly believe in. Yes, Dalí. Oh yes my brother…you are like pure magnetism and like a good drug to me.

Narrator :

And so it was that the artist started to walk the road to success. It would not take that long for the genius of Dalí to be recognized worldwide… becoming an indisputable and enigmatic legend.

1932- DIALOG BEWEEN DALI, GALA & BUÑUEL

Narrator :
After two films made by Luis Buñuel in which Salvador Dalí, at some
level was a collaborator in each movie, tension between the director
and the painter grew up to the point of distress. Gala could not help
being herself.

Buñuel :
Salvador listen to me, I have nothing to do with the results,
we were victims of opinions, abstract manipulations with financial
worries and tight budgets from people in a daily mood, rushing us,
looking to relief the fear and other circumstances with no clue of what
we did. I had the responsibility of making people to agree in giving
me the green light to finish on time the film. Nothing done has been
obscene.
Will you for once let me explain and please listen up...!

Gala :
Do you really want us to believe, that someone else
was wasting energy to obscure Salvador? Yes, my Salvador Dalí,
the man who gave you so many ideas for the scenes that you have
filmed and from what we are seeing now, he could not get the
recognition he deserves?
You are the one who placed him in a basket, to be rotten and ignored
from the film-making decisions of the great monsieur Buñuel.
You are despicable, and from now on we want nothing to do with
you. Go to hell....

Dalí :
I have to agree with Gala,
the movies were as much mine as they were yours.
And my name, not appearing in the film credit, I call it an act of
indecency; that, I shall never forget!

Buñuel :

Salvador, my dear friend. Gala is a manipulator, she has twisted the whole thing. Can't you see it...? Forget all about her... please!
I am taking responsibility, for what has happened. I will make it up to you. Forgive me. Just think of yourself with me as you always did.

Dalí :

Not much is to be forgiven, nor is there anything to be explained.
Not to you, I trusted you when I thought you were my friend.
We were true collaborators, professionals of our craft.
All the time we spent together, makes me feel I've been betrayed, and your presence I regret.
Gala is always on my side by providing harmony.
You are a selfish communist.
C'mon Gala, let us leave!

Narrator:

And that was about the end of a great friendship between Salvador Dalí and Luis Buñuel, before the delight of Gala, who knew better for herself.

1932- DIALOG BETWEEN SALVADOR DALI & ANDRE BRETON

Narrator :

Europe has been inundated with a huge wave of intellectual voices much more different from the past, especially in France, where big names and artist of all types were jacking for position to become leaders of the already established "school of surrealism." 1924- 1929 is the period of time where a long list of poets and writers, painters and artist at large, adhere to the fashionable surrealist art. Poet André Breton is the most visible head of the pack.

Breton :

I believe I am the leader, I gave myself to the movement,
I wrote my own manifesto, I am backed by many who support my own beliefs, but you, Salvador Dalí... what do you have to offer besides a long list of nonsense...?

Dalí :

Listen André, I will never take you seriously, even though you claim to be the founder of surrealist art, you and your colorless verses want to define an idea if not to capture the essence of surrealism... and that, should be up to me. It is that simple... my friend.

Breton : Oh sure! I heard that you often say to be proud of being a genius. You and the weight of your self- imposed aura, no more than a gift from Gala to you.
Who do you think that you are...? You are nothing but a non French lusting for prestige with colorful and blasphemous paintings.
You resemble a phony surrealist, obscene and lacking a sense of décor to say the least.

Dalí : Excuse me.... just look at me closely.

Breton :
For most of us you are vulgar and your presence is embarrassing. Our movement is supported by great artists,
we are writers and good thinkers; you have nothing to share with us.
We are the true surrealists and the cream of our art.

Dalí :
Wait a minute André. You and your band of followers may be the first at the finish line, but I am the best of all painters, because the others are bad. Besides you see me as an intruder causing fear in the ranks. Yes you do!
And if that is not enough, listen up! I will hold surrealism as the banner of my craft. And we all shall see to that....
If you like it or not.

Breton : There we go again, you and your true narcissism. You never give up. Do you?

Dalí :
You don't seem to slow down either. You, the author of two manifestos already, plus the one written by your enemy, yes, the poet Ivan Goll, and by the way... you know that his gang do not agree with you at all. You have divided the movement without scruples and not a good reason, but now... oh yes... now you are keeping me in mind.
Maybe Paul Eluard is jealous of me for having taken his wife.
I know that Paul has been and he still is on your side.

Breton :
You are out of your mind...!
I would gladly give you two francs so that you could disappear from our sight. As a matter of fact, as the leader of surrealism, that I am.
I am seriously considering erasing your name for life, from the list
of illustrious individuals who perform well in the surrealist art...
not an artist of despicable behavior and an annoying attitude
from someone like you.

Dalí :

Bravo…! Bravisimo …! Monsieur Breton.

Your impulse is wrong again, your words match the thickness of your brain and you simply cannot see beyond the tip of your nose.

You do not know who I am. No Sir, at least, not yet.

Some day you will regret this moment.

Breton : Yes I am sure. You go on.

Narrator :

By 1933 the name Salvador Dalí was stricken from the list of surrealist artist. That was not a detriment for the painter. Salvador Dalí knew that his madness as an artist had no barriers. At the end he proved everyone with conviction enough, that painters also could serve well in the surrealist school and not simply with thoughts and words from ideas of the surrealist wisdom as the system was originally conceived.

1934- DIALOG BETWEEN GALA AND HER DAUGHTER CECILE

Narrator :
The relationship between Salvador Dalí and Gala has taken a new
level. It seems there is no way but moving forward for the new couple.
Gala and Cecile (her daughter from a previous marriage to French
poet Paul Eluard) exchange words....

Cecile :
Mother... I wish I could call you mother with feelings out of my
heart.
The truth is that all this time we have been different people
living in different places, being uniquely apart.
You've been always out of sight. You have not been in my life.
I simply do not know you. I cannot tell who you are.

Gala :
Cecile... you are my natural daughter and there is nothing to change
that.
    You are a beautiful creature yet I can't be by your side.
Life have turned things up side down all around us.
Now I'm married to a man who loves me, cares for me,
a man bending over daily taking care of my needs;
and I must stay with him.

Cecile :
Oh mother... you and your Spanish painter.... never made me feel at
ease.
If it weren't for my father, by now, where would I be?
I know that you see it different, since I don't count in your life,
That is the way I always feel... I know I am rejected by you.

Gala : Cecile... life is not an easy thing; I did not mean to abandon
you, and I accept what I did while ignoring all your needs.

Yes, in the selfish attempt to stick to my only desires and dreams
I lost control and you babe, but I need you to understand that the
person that I am... I still need to be.

Cecile :

But mother... I am hurt and very much resentful.
What you are saying right now, I cannot even believe it is happening
to me.

It is not easy to accept the way that I am being rejected,
but I wish you well and happy, just the way you wish to live.

Gala :

Cecile... I don't know what else to say....but, I love you in my own
way and I want the best for you... I have always known that you
would be much better off with your father.
You truly deserve him and I wish you a healthy and good- long- life.

Narrator :

Cecile Eluard lived to be 99 years and was able to witness the early
years of the XXI century.

1936 - SALVADOR & GALA HEARD THE NEWSS ABOUT LORCA

Narrator : The early summer months of 1936 were a pleasant time for Salvador and Gala. Both were happily married and touring France while eagerly promoting his new paintings.

At the same time social turmoil and a big political storm is making its way throughout Spain. The tragedy of a bloody civil war is just about to get started. Away from it all, Dalí and Gala keep in touch with their folks back at home. They realize that while being safe in France, things would be more than positive for the artist and Gala knows how to take advantage of her husband's success in the arts.

Gala :
Look Salvador, excuse me but a telegram just came for you. It must be important. Would you like to open it now?

Dalí :
Yes… please let me see, this could be another order for a new painting. You know I am
good, but really I cannot keep up with so much work. Oh well let us see what they want.

Narrator :
With impatience Salvador read the words while suddenly turning pale, speechless and out of balance, he looked for a nearby chair

Dalí :
Oh… No… please no…! This is not true… It did not happen. It is impossible…! He is so young. This cannot be. What a tragedy. Oh nooooooooooooo.

Gala : Salvador calm down. It cannot be that bad. Just take a deep breath and please tell me what is wrong…! Let me see the telegram.

Dalí :

Oh Gala, this is about Federico. It cannot be... not him...! It is no way that my Federico is no longer alive. This is not a real telegram. It says that: Federico was detained and shot to death near his home town. It has been confirmed by newspapers in Madrid. How could this be? He never hurt anyone, he is a poet, an artist, a man of peace and one of the best among us. He even told me not to worry about him, for "no one kills poets." This is not real. I need to talk to Pablo Picasso, maybe he knows something different.

Gala :

Indeed this is sad. But yes getting in touch with Picasso sounds like a good idea, I really do not want to see you like this, but right now, just come to my arms and let me hold you tight. Breathe slowly, yes weep if you so desire my adorable Salvador.

Narrator :

Unfortunately the tragic news of the assassination of Federico García Lorca spread out as quickly as black powder thought Europe. With his death came the dismembering of he fiber of most Spanish intellectuals in and out of Spain. In the case of Dali as well as Picasso, since they were already immersed in the French culture of the days, both kept alive the amazing art galleries with the objects of their craft. Salvador Dali was enjoying being himself and began to believe in his role on Earth as a true genius, a magnificent surrealist. He and his art started to soar even higher.

1938- SALVADOR DALI MEETS WITH Dr. FREUD

Narrator :
By the time that Salvador Dalí was nothing but a straggling artist, Sigmund Freud was already a significant figure among his peers. The Austrian born, father and practitioner of psychoanalysis had become a refugee in England at the beginning of WWII. By now Salvador Dalí was establishing himself as a sought after painter, acquiring international fame and a surprising demand for his works.

He was also making money while suffering from his long time dreams, nightmares, neurosis, and obsessions close to despair; the symptoms from the subconscious. The artist decided to take time off to meet with Dr. Freud and learn from him. The meeting took place at the residence of Dr. Freud, over a cup of tea and the help of a translator between the two personalities.

Dr. Freud :
So you are Salvador Dalí...? I am happy to meet you! Since you appear to be doing so well, now you can tell me about your feelings, emotions, or whatever comes to mind.

Dalí :
Thank you Dr. Freud. I am just honored to meet you Sir. I have read most of your teachings. Your reputation is admirable and well deserved, I presume.

Dr. Freud :
 You presume...? It is funny, I do also presume about many things I see. Mostly the people I meet. By the way... would you care for some tea...?

Dalí : Yes of course, as long as it is hot, or at least, warm. You know how damp and cold it is out there, in the street. Besides, surrealism must be maintained at a constant temperature. That is according to me. But it is only my opinion. You may have your own opinions. Do you?

Dr. Freud :
I do, indeed, like many other secrets of my profession. You understand that. Do you?

Dalí :
I do Dr. Freud, as I told you I am an admirer of your work, although I always seek for more answers.

Narrator :
The conversation did not appear to go anywhere. With intensity and looks of curiosity both men were sizing up each other's egos. Each one for a reason of his own. The presence of that attitude did not make it easy for the translator, who kept trying his very best in order to maintain reason.

Freud was not impressed with the demeanor of the artist and Dalí started to look for an opportunity to end his visit.

Dalí :
Yes Dr. Freud… It has been an honor having exchanged words with you.

Dalí :
And I do appreciate your visit. Now, thank you and have a good day!

Narrator :
Nevertheless the influence of Dr. Freud rationalization in writing… had provided an explanation for many of the paintings by the surrealist artist. Freud's ideas and theories were taken to another level in order to bring the world of dreams, visions and unconscious images to a tangible reality; the surrealist paintings of Dalí.
From 1940 and on, Salvador Dalí was already capitalizing on the teachings of Freud and as a surrealist painter, he mastered his waves

of ability to create art into a collection of outstanding masterpieces for the world to see and admire.

1945-1946- DALI IS RETURNING TO SPAIN (dialog with Gala)

Narrator :

Early in 1945 the allied troops in Europe were putting a mortal dent in the Nazis strong holds. The free world was smelling its way to victory in WW II. The painter and his wife have residing in the U.S. for some time, they have faithfully followed the results of the war by the press. Now Dalí is thinking about where to travel next.

Dalí :

I find it hard to believe that the Germans have lost. I always knew that in life anything is possible, but Hitler's failure is a lot to swallow. I am convinced that Europe will be changing and I am not sure to what extend or how long it will take. I may be wrong, although rarely am.

Gala :

I told you so… The Russian army has done a good job. Besides that mad man of yours was not a genius. That is obvious.

Dalí :

Please Gala, do not use that title for the Fuhrer. The genius is within me and don't you forget it. The Nazis just did not have any luck. By the way, I am caressing the idea of going back to Spain. That crazy civil war has been over for some time now, and things are under control with general Franco.

Gala :

Salvador… are you out of your mind? Franco is another dictator, in charge of the will of the people…. Is that what you want for us? Do you…? Besides, you know what they say about the prophets not being so in their home land. You will not be treated as you are here in the US. Also your father is gone and our place in Cadaques may not exist anymore. Write to your dear sister, and she will confirm that. I am not sure that returning to Spain is a good idea at this time.

Dalí :

Oh no Gala, I have to disagree with you. I don't pretend to be a prophet nor do I have to prove myself to be the artist that I am, but I have a vision and I see myself embarked on the vessel of success, right in my home land.

I believe I will be accepted and I also feel the urge to be there, to sink my feet in the sand, the beaches I missed so much. I want to add a twist to my new creations, make myself similar to the classics, but exquisite and unique. Yes, the touch of Dalí blending with the best surrealism ever dreamed in the world.

Gala:

Oh well, you are the artist and I will follow your instinct. Just one thing: keep in mind that the money is not in Spain. At least not in the arts.

Dalí :

I care not about money. You do Gala, and if we make it over there, I know that I will, you shall be there with me, and having total command.

We shall continue being two great people in demand and the world will not cease for us.

People will beg for more of Dalí and a castle I shall build for you to reign as my queen. C'mon Gala let's pack up.

Narrator :

In 1948 Dalí and Gala arrived in Spain, establishing residence in the small Mediterranean coastal town of Port Lligat, a quiet place very close to the old family house where he grew up in Cadaques. There, by the beach, the painter would spend over thirty years of his life and continue to produce and sell world renowned paintings that made him larger than life.

1947- SALVADOR DALI AND HIS CATHOLIC FAITH

Narrator : *Born and raised in a traditional Catalan-Spanish family, Salvador Dalí grew up knowing the teachings of the Catholic Church. His mother, Doña Felipa, was very influential to him and his father was the authority of the home. For one reason or another, always with a mind of his own, young Dalí gradually grew away from the formalities of the faith. To the dislike of his parents he started to show no interest in organized religion. As an adult, with a questionable personal behavior, he was considered by many, including his family, to be a man of no morals and in the eyes of the church a person living in sin.*

That was never an impediment for the artist. He simply could not care less. In his pursuit of greatness, notoriety and fame came easy to him. However the artist knew very well the classic painters of the Renaissance and their successful association with themes of religion. Besides, Michael Angelo and Rafael were among the idols for the Spanish master of surrealism. Even Pablo Picasso had performed in 1930 a superb painting of the Crucifixion and Salvador Dalí wanted to be in the good graces with everyone, including the Catholic Church.

The genius of Dalí had already experimented with new creations and survived the heavy criticism for having portrayed on canvas the face of Gala as Virgin Mary. Sacrilegious to some, or a great piece of art for others, the best religious paintings were yet to come.In 1947 Dalí and Gala were promoting some new works in France. The artist was still caught in his owns nightmares while dealing with life and the subconscious. He felt being possessed by the devil, harassed and tormented in his nightly sleep. Dalí truly believed in Gala as the muse of his artistic creations, and yet he seemed to be aware of some outside force with powers affecting his artistic vision while eroding his soul. An Italian friar Gabriele Maria Berardi is believed to have come to the rescue and performed an exorcism at the artist's request.

That is what it was said and spreader around time, for the artist never denied it nor confirmed such an act.

The friar always claimed that after the exorcism, Dalí became free from the demons and as a form of compensation, the artist handed to him a sculpture of the Christ on the Cross. A gift that the friar proudly displayed letting people know the story behind that precious work of art. Some decades later, both, the artist and the friar were no longer alive. The cross was found in the state of the friar and some experts on the works of Dalí, claimed that it was without a doubt a job completed by the Spanish artist around mid XX century.

With or without an exorcism, Salvador Dalí became even more attracted to religious themes, always combining his unique style with the flavor of the classics. The result is a great collection of paintings that brought some members of the Catholic Church closer to the artist. Even the Pope (Pius XII) was able to concede a special audience in the Vatican to the couple of society's moment : Dalí and Gala. Without question, the taste of the artist, touch of color and attention to detail became another credential for all "Dalí' religious paintings" while establishing the artist's reputation as a classical artist of modern art. Some fine examples of religious paintings are listed below:

- *The temptation of St. Anthony -1946*
- *The Madonna of Port Lligat -1949*
- *Christ of St. John of the Cross -1951*
- *Crucifixion/ Corpus Hyparabus -1954*
- *The last supper -1955*
- *Virgin of Guadalupe -1959*
- *The discovery of America by Christopher Columbus - 1959*
- *Ecumenical council -1960*
- *Sacred heart of Jesus Christ -1962*

And many more paintings of that nature....

The names of the famous paintings listed above are just a short selection of titles in the long list of master pieces by Salvador Dalí. They all are housed and exhibited with joyful reverence in different public or private collections in places all over the world.

1948- DALI AND GALA ARRIVED TO SPAIN WITH WEDDING PLANS

Narrator :

By 1948 Dalí and Gala have decided to fulfill the artist's wish of returning to his home land, Spain. Both are at middle aged and enjoying good health. So far all the artistic endeavors have proved to be successful for Dalí and his wife. Both find themselves contemplating the future with energy and their eyes wide open for a life that keeps smiling at them. At least in their own way.

Dalí :

I am able to feel having made the right decision. We are here, in my home land and definitely to stay. From here we shall create art like only Dalí could dream it. We shall go out and mingle with the powers that be. They all will find out that I am true surrealism, even in my own country.

Gala :

I believe you Salvador... but you do not have to go anywhere to prove to anyone who you are... what you are made of... or the fact that you belong on the top podium of the arts. I will be with you applauding the greatness of your beliefs. You have always been the best surrealist with an exceptional mind.

Dali :

Yes Gala, I know what you mean by that, and I appreciate your words.

Narrator :

Definitely the couple found the peace of mind they were looking for, at the same time, both were enjoying the acceptance of the country's political establishment and a growing admiration if not veneration of others involved in the arts in and out of the Spanish borders. Once they were settled near the birthplace of the painter, they were content with the life style while more creations from the artist were up for display and sale. At the same time Dalí was seen holding hands with the fascist political system of the country as well as he gradually got closer to the return to his childhood Catholic faith. At least on appearance.

Art exhibits were increasingly in demand everywhere and Dalí was able to deliver. Yet, he felt the urge of adding a new dimension to his artistic creation on canvas. Religious themes were created becoming classics and without question very much in the line of the great traditional school of Spanish painting, only this time with the indisputable touch of Salvador Dalí.

Dalí :
I feel caught at a crossroad between soul and body, the divine and the human, spiritualism and materialism, heaven and earth and yet, I cannot be satisfied till I add color to my agonizing desire to fulfill... all of my dreams.
There is something in my inside telling me how to act next. I am thinking of having a church wedding. You and me before the altar. That would add flavor and more prestige to
our marriage in front of society and of course, the rest of the world.

Gala :
But Salvador, please do not make me laugh, that is nonsense. You think such a wedding will make you change and fulfill your marital rights. C'mon and be serious, we have been married for years now, yes it was a civil ceremony, but a wedding nevertheless. Besides, there are difficulties in the Catholic Church. You know... here, they will make it impossible for us , especially for me. I have never cared much about that sort of organized religion, and now less than ever, that is me. We are married and you know it well.

Dalí :
Listen Gala, our marriage in Spain took place before the civil war and as such, at the present time, it is not valid in the eyes of Franco's government. If we are going to live here, we have to do it the right way, at least in the eyes of people who don't seem to stop following

us. In addition to that, I seem to be in the good graces of the actual political establishment, and that favors my trajectory as an acclaimed citizen and an artist with a name of international fame. We need to get married in the church. But first we are going to need a papal dispensation...maybe a trip to the Vatican will help. Oh yes once we are married in the church... things will go smooth for all of us.

Gala :
I do not care for your government's stupid laws nor the church you suddenly so strongly seem to admire. I have been married twice already. Standing by your side, and knowing to be your muse, it is all I need. We are doing fine the way we are. Let it be for now... and see what happens next. Then again, If I listen to your instinct we could play along and beat them at their own game. After all, what can we lose? Gala and Dalí are meant to be one inseparable team. You as the artist and me as your muse.

Dalí :
Now you are making sense, my dear Gala, you keep up with my desires and a castle I shall build you. Yes my dear, just for you, I will be happy to share a fortune at your command and of course I shall provide you with prestige for being the wife of "an uncontested surrealist of divine craziness." Yes that is me, the great Salvador Dalí.

Gala :
Oh Salvador Dalí, you never stop to amazing me. Oh by the way, we have already sold your latest work, so that you know. What is the theme of your new painting...?

Narrator :
It was 1957 and after a presumable list of political contacts, paper work and a hard to understand papal dispensation, the wedding took place in the Roman Catholic Church between Salvador Dali and Gala. Neither were very spiritual souls and their matrimonial farce continued till death took them apart. For personal reasons and other issues out of tune, children never appear in their marriage. Only Gala's daughter Cecile from a previous marriage prevailed but always in the distance, in France.

1949- ANA MARIA SISTER OF DALI

Narrator:

Ana María Dalí was a beautiful young girl, growing up with her brother Salvador, under their parents roof. She always said that her brother, behaved candid with multiple signs of attentions for her. Since they were the only two children in the family, that certainly made her to feel more than special.

She always said that his brother acted so serious that he found time just for nothing that was not the new painting on his mind. Since his initial attempt to use the canvas and practice with colors, he showed all and convinced them that he was an artist. The mother of Salvador, Felipa, was very happy to see that. And so was the artist's father, also named Salvador.

Ana María used to watch her brother like he were hypnotized at least chained to his obsession. Soon she was asked to model, that was more than a thrill. She felt important standing in front of the window overlooking at the beach. Ana Maria become the muse and unique model for her brother. The paintings took place in the second floor of the house, and the room being used by Salvador, became the painting studio for the young artist.

Such a tranquil atmosphere and so much absorbing time that it was.

Salvador took care of details by enhancing her figure, the hair and both arms. He himself was so pleased with the results that many more paintings came up giving life to Ana María, some becoming classics in the painter's catalog.

After the death of her mother she became the kind of surrogate mother and the pillow for her brother. They were always very close and the modeling continue for the artist in the family that seem to bring pride to all.

Life went on and her modeling career ended by the time Dalí, met almost out of nowhere, the woman that changed his life, Gala.

Ana María accepted the fact that her brother was not going to return to being the man she has known and adored....
Life went on for everyone, especially for the painter with his colors, objects, human faces and geometrical forms always catered by his Gala who kept him moving along.

By 1947 the artist's sister became vey much enchanted with the arrival to town of her brother and her wife. By this time Dalí was famous and the recognition for his work was international. Things could be positive once more for the family. She wrote the biography of her brother in 1949. She called the book: "Dalí seen by her sister." Not a great literary piece but a tribute to an established artist who at that time he had almost forty more years to go in life.

1950- DALI AND HIS TWO MADONNAS OF PORT LLIGAT

Narrator :
One could never understand the state of mind of Dalí's personality. He has already proven to be a true artist of unique ideas in the school of Symbolism, Cubism and of course Surrealism, and why not, classical forms. At this time of his life, he wanted to demonstrate that he could do it all. There is no reason to question his ability as a painter of style, once again, and while using his wife as a model and the muse she became in his life, he created some unexpected new paintings of religious flavor.

Gala :
Oh my dear Salvador I know that these days you seem to be contemplating the idea of caressing religious subjects for your work. Well go ahead. Why don't you use me as the Mother of Jesus? I would not mind it at all and you certainly will enjoy this new challenge of yours. I will be by your side, and you know it.

Dalí :
Once again you are able to convince me, Gala. You read well my mind and I shall pick up my tools to get started right now. Of course, you shall be in the painting just as you so desire. Let's go…!

Gala :
That is the artist you are… a genius with energy and vitality like no one. Frankly I cannot find adjectives to describe the geniality of your work. I know that you will master this new painting and amaze the world with it. By the way Salvador, should I pose standing up or just sitting on this chair…?

Narrator :
The artist followed his natural instinct and at last he began to feel in touch with his soul, accompanied by that religious flavor self put

aside from his life for a long time. This time using the face of Gala, in 1949 he started to paint an interesting piece where his wife would represent the Virgin Mary, being seated while holding in her lap the baby Jesus. The background would show Mediterranean waters and clouds from their beloved living place of Port LLigat a little town on the Catalan coast, in the northeast of the Iberian Peninsula, Spain.

Dalí :
It is finished. I will call it The Madonna of Port Lligat. I am sure that somebody will have something to say about it. It is natural, but as long as I am the genius I am, I can make the trip to the Vatican, and guess what ? I would even present this painting to the Pope.

Gala :
And why not? Salvador, I am proud of you, I am very pleased. This is something unique. I love your idea, but first sign this new masterpiece of yours. That is important.

Narrator :
This new work of art "The Madonna of Port Lligat" became a subject of controversy. Everyone had an opinion about the painting. The artist was labeled to exhibit bad taste with his nonsense and sinful behavior; even blasphemy. Others thought otherwise.
Yet, Salvador Dalí and his wife made the pilgrimage to Rome and Pope Pius XII did approve the painting for the couple. Not too many people were prepared for that sort of papal response. The Holly Father had made his point, but many Catholics were openly offended and critics never ceased to talk about it. Nevertheless, The Madonna of Port Lligat as a painting became internationally popular. Nowadays, that piece of art is still revered as a classic and it resides in an art gallery in Milwaukee, Wisconsin, USA.

Dalí :
Gala I told you. We have acquired one more success and you are my muse and unique model. I truly feel compelled to paint one more Madonna of Port Lligat. I will maintain the same theme with you as the protagonist and holding the infant Jesus, only this time I will add

as background some new features with colorful details of surrealist flavor.

Narrator :

This new painting and second "Madonna of Port Lligat" created in 1950, even though it was similar to its predecessor (only one year earlier) became an irresistible piece of art in high demand. Presently it resides in a prestigious art gallery in Japan.

There were many more paintings to come where Gala was represented as "Mary." So it happened in 1954 with the classic "The Crucifixion Hypercube" where Gala stands at the base of the cross, or "The Ecumenical Council." This last painting, like many others, became another successful story in 1960.

For some it was a continuous sinful attempt to insult and provocation. For others it was and still remains art at its best.

1960- BUÑUEL RETURNS TO SPAIN AND WISHES TO MEET DALI

Narrator :
By this time Salvador Dalí is an artist of international dimensions. He and his wife are doing extremely well in business He is totally accepted as a celebrity.

Somehow he is aware of the possibility of a new movie being filmed in Spain. A movie to be done with a director he knew from the past.

Dalí :
Impossible, this won't happen in Spain. Not in this country while Franco is in charge. Luis Buñuel is a consummate communist and he will never set foot again on this land.

Narrator :
The Spanish government still under the consequences of its civil war (1936-1939) has already prohibited Luis Buñuel from entering his native country. By now leaving in exile due to his revolutionary ideas as a self proclaimed communist while remaining a well established movie director of international acclaim.

Through a lot of political maneuvering and extra money passed along... Buñuel is given special permission to stay in the country for a short time, under police vigilance during the filming of scenes, especially the exterior around a small town in Toledo. This production would be one of his finest master pieces on film: Viridiana was a movie packed with renowned stars involved in a story mastered by Luis Buñuel. The film came to be a classic in the cinematography culture. The cinematographer also wanted to use this opportunity to find his old pal Salvador Dalí.

Buñuel :
Hello Pepín... this is me Luis, yes Luis Buñuel. It has been a long time! You know, I am so happy to hear your voice again. You seem to be doing well and joyful as ever. By the way. Have you heard from Salvador lately? I also read the press and he seems to be capitalizing in his art.

Pepín :
Well, thank you Luis... yes I have heard from Salvador from time to time. But you know that since he got married he is tied up to Gala. Besides he does not speak too much about himself and he lives up close to Barcelona. I am still in Madrid. It is a long trip as you can realize.

Buñuel :
I personally would love to see you and if Salvador is there, that would be even better. As far as Gala is concerned... I always wanted to strangle her. I am sure that for all of us it would be like in the old days, but my moves around here are limited since the police keep an eye on me all the time. Some things never change. Right now I am busy with the filming of what will be Viridiana and I am thrilled with everyone around me. You know it is a great story to tell, this time on film.

Pepín :
You are right Luis, I know that you shall do fine and I wish you success too. By all means we shall be in touch.

Narrator :
The movie was completed by 1961, but its released in Spain was forbidden. Even the Vatican said that the film was blasphemous. The French had no problem with it and in the Cannes Festival, Viridiana won the prestigious Palm D'OR.

Luis Buñuel just did it again and his trajectory as a film maker made him bigger. Later on Salvador Dalí confessed that he would have made the trip to Cannes and congratulate the director in person, but that did not take place. It is believed that Gala had something to do with it.

1968- DALI AND GALA ENJOY THE FRUITS OF THEIR LABOR

Narrator :

In life, very few artist have been able to make a living while performing and selling their creations. Good painters have never been an exception, especially when looking for some well deserved recognition while they were performing and striving to make it. By the mid sixties Dalí and Gala were enjoying the fruits of the painter's labor.

Dalí :

I see myself being a truly successful artist, but I am not done. Not yet. Last night I had one more dream and today I will finish it with colors over a new canvas, simply waiting to become another gift to humanity from the genius I posses. It is a pleasure to wake up every morning and realize that I am Salvador Dalí.

Gala :

Yes. You go on, but make sure that you sign it. Yes the painting! Remember: just your signature is worth millions my dear. By the way there are some friends coming to visit today. Do not bother to come, or interrupt our party, unless you prefer to be part of the game. Like I said, your signature is important. Oh yes my dear... I love you and I always will, but now I have to go....

Narrator :

Dalí was busier than ever producing master pieces, attending media interviews on radio and TV, the gossip magazines were not an exception. Yet his popularity was packed with rumors about his personal life, his likes and dislikes were frequently displayed in an open window for all to see, often taking away the merits from the artist. Dali was a mystery. In the eyes of many, perhaps a crazy man. Meanwhile Gala was the lady she always wanted to be: free to exercise her desires. The personal parties she used to arrange with people not associated with Dalí, became the talk of the town. Most often, Dalí had other things in his mind.

Dalí :
One more painting to my credit, it is done and sold for two million pesetas. Right Gala? You know I have no idea of how much money that is… but we need to get ready for an upcoming event in Paris, then to London and back to the New York. The telegram says it is urgent and I wish not to be a deterrent to my fans.

Gala :
Oh yes. Speaking of deterrent… what ever happened to that castle you were going to build for me? Salvador, you know that the way I am… I always fall in love with your delightful ideas and pleasant surprises.

Dalí :
Soon Gala, very soon I shall provide with the keys to your castle. I have made arrangement with the architects and my own design plans will suit your needs and good taste. After all, you are with me, you are my shadow, my muse. You will see that it will happen upon our return from overseas. Gala trust me, first is first and now we ought to get ready to catch the next flight to Paris.

Gala : Yes … and I guess. Meantime I shall be patient, but I cannot wait to hold the keys in my hands so that I can open the door to my own castle.

Narrator :
And so it was that by1969, the castle of Pubol was almost ready for the new owners. An old medieval mansion totally enlarged and renovated inside, became the Castle of Pubol. Residence of Gala for most of the year and decorated to her liking and for her own pleasures, whatever they were.

Dalí himself agreed to his wife's request to not visit the castle while she was inside the ne residence, she meant without written permission, signed by his her and only her. He acted as agreed and never tried to change her mind. At the death of Gala she was buried inside the castle where she remains today.

The town of Pubol still keeps the castle intact and it is open to the public. The few curious that visit such as emblematic site, find "The Gala-Dalí Castle House Museum." Its location is in a small quiet Catalan town, several miles north of Barcelona, and relatively close to the mountains of the Pyrenees.

1975- LATE YEARS DIALOG BETWEEN GAL AND DALI

Narrator :
At the end of their lives the relationship between Gala and Dalí... did not go exactly smooth. Gradually it became a bumpy road due to the daily erosion and disbelief from both sides.

Dalí :
You and your urging demands, you never seem to be satisfied... I'm beginning to feel tired and I think I had enough.

Gala:
Salvador, don't look at me as if I were the enemy.
C'mon now "painter of dreams..." or would you prefer the
the title of "painter of nightmares." Please grow up!
You are the one, who refuses to see things for what they are,
and not just the way you simply believe they ought to be.

Dalí :
Gala, listen to me... I have seen just about everything there is to exist, I've seen beyond the horizon that surrounds the fortune we have made.
   I witnessed others like leeches sucking us blood as we speak.
My eyes and hands feel too tired, I am lacking energy,
all I want from now on is to stop and enjoy life in contemplation,
with no limits or bad dreams; no more fantasy.

Gala :
That is not you. You are Salvador Dalí, invincible and a pure example of surrealism at its best but an immortal species as long as you stay with me.
You will never get to exist without my breath on your neck, without my eyes on your hands while accepting who we are.
You go nowhere without me.

It is a delightful experience that I enjoy very much when I am able to wrap you with the chains of our destiny.

Yes Salvador, you do need me as much as you need a canvas before you can fall asleep… not to dream, but to keep painting; always driven by your divine fantasy.

Dalí :

Oh shut up. Now, I'm able see clear through your transparency. I can tell the shape and length of that crawling snake within you and I tell you that I am tired… please… just get away from me.

Gala :

No Salvador. You still think you are "a genius" but you are no much without me.

How could you just believe, that you could have ever made it on your own?

Think about it and you will see that… Oh… Oh… you've pushed me. Oh not again… You've hit me… You... you...

You crazy man. I am in pain, you S.O.B.

Narrator :

Rumors by servants in the house were leaked to the press. They all heard loud voices and discussions throughout the house when Gala and Dali were facing each other. Pity!

It did not take too long for her to suffer with pain the fracture of weak bones and a terrible infection though her body, much of it was conducive to her death. That was 1982. A quiet funeral took place and without fuss, her casket was taken to Castle Pubol. Her body still rests in the crypt and tomb built for her by her husband Salvador Dalí.

Buñuel :

Well, well, well…!

Gala is dead at last. Finally we don't have to worry any more about her, portraying virgin Mary. What a farce that she was, although I wonder if from the bottom of her tomb, she may still display some influence over the mind of Salvador. A man and a passionate artist, an old time friend who I respect and admire.

Narrator : Luis Buñuel outlived Gala, but for a short time, he died one year later in 1983.

1983- DALI'S FINAL THOUGHTS

Narrator :
Salvador Dalí loses his wife Gala in 1982 and he enters a deep stage
of depression that will last till his last days....

Dalí :
So Gala is not here... finally there is silence in the house,
but I am able to detect the shadow of her presence in every room.

Her breathing over my shoulders is a memory simply not going away,
when thinking about it, still makes me shiver.

Somehow she always knew how to make my moments vulnerable
to her liking, her devious taste and ambition sugar coated
with loving words towards me, were like venom.

Perhaps, I was blind to her ability to redirect my emotions
for the indifference I felt through the sequence of events
occurring over the years with the companions she kept.
That never ending whirlwind of insatiable sex addicts

I was trapped with, or amused by... I'm not sure anymore...!
Gala knew well I did not care much for her unusual habits
as long as I could feel her juices flowing among my creations;
allowing my daily dreams...
to blossom while I was happily asleep.

For me, money was never a motive to be driven to the market.
I've always known that the merchant that I was labeled to be
had no room in my ability to achieve the genius I am,
or should I say I became, because now I'm out of breath...
slowly approaching the end.

Narrator :

Soon after Gala's death, the painter lost faculties, and due to an accidental fire that took place in his home, Salvador Dalí spent time confined to a wheelchair with little or no contact with the outside world. He died in his long loved Spanish villa in 1989. His funeral was worldwide news and attended by thousands of people.

Even though we all accept being vulnerable in the face of death, it is easy to understand that Dalí's excellence as an artist, remains unequivocal and proud of him.

A PAINTER AMONG THE BEST

With a trace of self indulgence
multiple paintings were left
behind a master collection
of contemporary art.

Most of it… is surrealism
other pieces are cubism
not to mention the traditional colors
on prestigious canvas
enhancing history
even some religion's facts
based on fantasy in his mind.

It is not hard to accept
the fact that among great painters
Dalí is among the best
and as time is passing by there is no reason to test
his ability as an artist of profound deep interest.

UNDENIABLE DALI

Observing his paintings…
one is convinced that the genius was within a quick temper,
perhaps a bizarre thinking
being touched by a divine intervention, craziness from
a unique unconscious mind.

Always in the public opinion, and not to be put aside
he could not care less about what was said about him.

Dali was moved in one direction,
driven by his keen imagination;
the exclusive execution of his art
by producing master pieces that not too many could match.

His appearances all over were regarded as abstract
and yet he was interesting with comments to make us smile.

His paintings… there… they are…
unequivocal and undeniable from an artist and a man
who behaved by being indifferent to success right at his hand.

He could see the notoriety of his craft
and he knew how to make money
with help from his better half
that for about fifty years made all his dreams
to come true.

Something to say about that

SO MANY PIECES OF ART

So many pieces of art have replenished world-wide-galleries.
So many themes over the canvas have been produced
with splendor and geniality.
So much respect for the artist who brings life to the
images… not just with color, but taste.
There is so much to enjoy while admiring a good painting
that really touches the heart,
while we dream somehow pretending
if not wishing we could be
the ones behind such skill
and craftsmanship.
That is why it won't take much
to give up and surrender to the surrealistic dreams
produced by the eccentric thinking of one of the
greatest painters of the XX century.
Of course…! Salvador Dalí.
Yet I surely understand the fact, that by any reason,
you don't have to agree with me
but in Dalí I believe…!

SOME FAMOUS PHRASES & A SAMPLE OF HIS POETRY

Salvador Dalí was never considered to be a poet nor a philosopher, and yet his spontaneous answers over observations about life and himself... are phrases of poetic conviction to be taken seriously. He was definitely a thinker and a very sharp individual with a vision fully aware of his surroundings. The following are a few samples of his finest quotes:

- Intelligence without ambition is a bird without wings.
- I am not strange, I am just not normal.
- Everything alters me, but nothing changes me.
- I am surrealism.
- Those who do not want to imitate anything, produce nothing.
- Painting is an infinite part of my personality.
- Have no fear to perfection, you will never reach it.
- The secret of my influence has always been that it remained secret.
- The first man to compare the cheeks of a young woman to a rose, was obviously a poet. The first to repeat it, it was an idiot.
- The thermometer of success is merely the jealousy of the malcontents.
- I do not do drugs. I am drugs. / Take me, I am drugs.
- There are some days when I think I am going to dye from an overdose of satisfaction.
- Don't bother about being modern. Unfortunately it is the only thing that whatever you do. you cannot avoid.
- At age six I wanted to be a cook. At seven I wanted to be Napoleon. And my ambition has been growing steadily ever since.

- Remember that the Chinese revolution was not a peasants revolution, but one of the extreme right.
- Wars never hurt anyone, except the people who die.
- Sex is an illusion. The most exciting thing is not having sex.
- Surrealism is distractive, but it destroys only what it considers to be shackles limiting our vision.
- What it is important is to create confusion, and not to eliminate it.
- No movie can be made about the life of Dalí. It would be too long.

Dali became an author by writing some books, even his own biography. Being a man of words he dealt with poetry in his very unique way. Here is a poem that enhances his keen imagination with a sense of humor typical of his humorous craft :

Untitled poem:

> "I am afraid of being on this shore,
> a branchless trunk, and what I must regret
> is having no flowers, pulp or clay
> for the worms of my despair."

Untitled poem (in his native Spanish) :

> *"Siento miedo por estar en esta orilla,*
> *ser un tronco sin ramas, y lo que más siento es*
> *no tener flores, ni pulpo frutal o tierra*
> *para el gusano de mi desesperación."*

A SELECTION OF HIS FAMOUS PAINTINGS

Narrator :
It is not an easy task to prepare a list of selected paintings created by Salvador Dalí. He painted with substance, style and his own original ideas. Sometimes like a mad man, sometimes like a classic, but always like a Dalí. He used to say that "if you look at a painting of Velazquez... you will find a Velazquez and if you look at a Picasso you will find a Picasso, but while looking at a painting of Dalí... you will see nothing like Dalí." He was a versatile artist with over 1,500 paintings to his merit, the selection of this work is up to each individual and personal taste. In the modest opinion of this author, some of Dalí's best work can be found in paintings like...

- "Vilabertran" (1913) is an early painting of Salvador. Dali when he was no more than nine years old.
- "Port of Cadaqués" (1919)
- "Night Walking Dreams"(19222)
- "Cabaret Scene" - an experiment in cubism- (1922)
- "Woman at the Window" (1925)
- "The Basket of Bread" (1926)
- "Portrait of Paul Eluard" (1929)
- "The Great Masturbator" (1929)
- "The Persistence of Memory" (1931)
- "Soft Construction of Beans" (1936)
- "Dream Caused by the flight of a Bea" (1945)
- " Basket of Bread" (1946)
- "Leda Atomica" (1949)
- "Christ of Saint John of the Cross" (1951)

- "The Disintegration of Time" (1952)
- "The Colossus of Rhodas" (1954)
- "The Sacrament of the Last Supper" (1955)
- "The Discovery of America by Christopher Columbus" (1959)
- "The Ecumenical Council" (1960)
- "Portrait of my dead Brother" (1963)
- "Gala Contemplating the Mediterranean sea" (1970)
- "Gala- Elena Ivanovna Diakanova" (1972)
- "Femme a Tete de Rose" (1981)
- "The swallow's Tail" (1983) it is believed to be the last painting of Salvador Dalí.

Narrator :
This were just a few names of paintings among a large number of masterpieces he created for humanity.

Salvador Dalí also practiced sculpture. One of his many displays in bronze is the statue he prepared for his wife Gala and it is proudly displayed in the town of Marbella (Spain.) It is without question a magnificent prove of his many skills as an artist.

Other sides of his artistic talent were on display by his jewelry designs, commercials, graphic arts, interior/exterior decorations, furniture, window shop dressing solutions, many designs for commercial items and ideas for the movies. Oh yes and much more.

DALI – APOLITICAL AT ALL..? MAY BE

Narrator :

The young Salvador Dalí was not raised in a family breathing the political atmosphere of the days. After the defeat suffered in the Spanish American war and the loss of colonies overseas, Spain appeared to be calmed. The Dalí's family was comfortably settled and respected in town, yet his father knew what strings to pull with important people in the government. He never sided with anyone in particular, unless it was for personal convenience. Young Dalí grew up at ease, as a good catholic boy, without a worry in his mind, not even a simple interest for who was running the City Hall of his beloved town. Later on, as student in Madrid, he still could care less for who was involved in politics anywhere.

Salvador Dalí was in his twenties when an army general took charge as the new dictator of the nation. That was never a concern for Dalí, even though the country was sinking in a war in North Africa and young men were continuously sent over to fight. Dalí, while being enrolled as student at school in Madrid, he felt safe and away from any concern, but himself.

In those days to serve to Spain in military uniform was mandatory for all young men. So, once Dalí was out of school and still in military age, he was sent to serve the country in an army depot, that, to his advantage was located very close to his home town. Of course it worked out for Salvador Dali, he was discharged in less than one year. It is believed that his father's money had influenced someone in power. Dalí still did not care much for the leaders of the government and the word "patriotism" was not in the artist's vocabulary.
Later on in his late twenties, and being very much focused in his paintings, he met a Russian born married woman who soon forged Dalí with ideas to create a new life, suitable for both of them as a couple.

By that time Spain's dictatorship by the Army General Primo de Rivera and this successor General Berenguer were gone, and the new second Republic was born in 1931. Dalí took advantage of the circumstances, that for instance allowed him to marry a divorcee; in a civil ceremony. Art was also encouraged and in some cases supported by the government. Dalí was content with that environment. Soon after, things got complicated in the political arena of Spain. By 1936 a new civil war broke up. The painter and his wife were already connected with a network of international artists and business people much interested in art. Besides, as some said once about Dalí: his behavior resembles a motor always running in high gear."

Dalí stayed away from the two sides fighting a war in his home land. He was definitely making it with his artistic style, and fame was at the doorstep of his works. Actually and knowing that his blood family were still at home, his decision to remain far and away from all was shared by his wife Gala. The war in Spain ended in 1939, but Dalí remained in foreign land; taking sides with no one.

It did not take much longer for WW II to commence. By that time, the artist, was well established in France. Once again the Dalít was not to be found at the site of war. He and his wife run for cover to the U.S. It seems like wherever he was, he could just smell trouble coming up. Pitty!

At the time it was said, that even though the couple (Dalí and Gala) were away from that terrible war, they truly believed that Nazi Germany would easily win the war. They both made comments about it and felt very strong about the outcome of WW II. After all, Dalí was a sympathizer of Hitler, by admiring his mannerisms, defiance and demeanor in front of the rest of the world.

At the end, the artist and his wife surely have to face the musical surprise of victory for the allied troops. Once the war was over and the waters of peace were at the level of the painter's likes, the couple made arrangements in order to program changes in the future of their lives.

So happened that back to Spain, Salvador Dali became a supporter of the political regime under general Franco. All of the sudden, the artist full of energy and ambition sought to stayed in the good graces with the Generalissimo, the new dictator of his country. This was much in favor of most of Spain's government. They all saw in Dalí a brilliant opportunity to be shared with the rest of the world. Things worked out for both: the artist using his homeland as a personal, desirable international platform, and Spain's cultural growth due to the fame of Salvador Dalí.

Dalí and Gala were not practicing Catholics and though they were married in a civil ceremony, long time ago, that was considered to be a clear sin in the eyes of the Spanish Church of the days. Even so, the couple was accepted when requesting a petition for a religious wedding ceremony. For one reason or another, they also were received in the Vatican with the blessings of Pope Pius II.
It was observed and alleged that the artist only pledged his allegiance to his wife Gala, his work; the art he created so well. Everything else, like establishments, politics or religion, became vehicles to ride through the highway of success. And so he was a force to recon with.

THE MOUSTACHE, SIGNATURE AND TITLES OF RECOGNITION

Narrator : Although Dalí, as a young man displayed a fashionable trimmed moustache, he shaved it off and grew it on simply to please his mood. However as time went on and his notoriety as a painter become an obvious highway of success, he decided to add something to his facial image, something that would make him look different from the rest. Or at least, that is what he thought of.

His curly and waxed moustache became an iconic trademark in the appearance of the artist. Flamboyant and much to the image and style of another Spanish master painter of the 17th century. It was the revered Diego Velázquez who influenced Dalí not only to paint but how to proudly display such a dignifying moustache for the rest of his life.

His signature *became a trademark and a recognizable icon among followers and, lovers of the arts, even for thieves trying to capitalized by committing forgery and cheat Dalí out of his fortune.*

The honorable titles received in his home land were several :

1964 - Knight Grand Cross of the Order of Isabel the Catholic.

1972 - Associate member of the Royal Academy of Science, letters & Fine Arts of Belgium

1981 - Knight Grand Cross of the Order of Charles III of Spain.

1982 - 1st Marqués de Dalí de Púbol, title given to the painter by King Juan Carlos of Spain.

Also the French Government recognized him with titles like :

• Member of the Legion of Honor of France.

• Associate member of the Academie dex Beaux-Arts of the Institut of France.

HIS LEGACY

Narrator : Dalí once said: "I myself am surrealism." With a sort of smile, one could go along with it or find an argument about that statement. The truth is that Dalí always enjoyed being seen as a surrealist.

His bizarre, even alleged not normal behavior going along with his works, made him a cultural icon and a subject of controversy. Although his personal life as a human being is as much debatable as disturbing, he could be easily excused from it, since he was always a mystery in front of his fellow man. He proudly stood by the fact that his personal life... was no one's business.

Even today, many people believe that his life was a fantasy, a dream, an aberration, even a show or an experience packed with surprises to many... that is up to personal interpretation. In his own time, Dalí became a provocative and enigmatic force to be reckoned with, especially by making some people to wonder and comment about his ability to lead, he was able to deliver withal his artistic creations.

One could say that he was a controversial individual, a man with a big ego, pure madness with no limits. Out of logic or genius, Dalí was for sure an interesting character, adding color to his image of arrogance and why not... great talent. Without question... he was a man with an exceptional mind.

Thinking positive, and framing him as the crazy artist that he was, he became a legend in his own time, a millionaire artist, a teacher, a leading man, a showman, but most of all, he definitely came to be an inspiration to many modern artists, yes including the surrealists .

All throughout his life, the artist appeared to be convinced that his presence on Earth had a purpose. He even believed that he was the reincarnation of his older brother, who had died at an early age. However and without question, Dalí and his wife Gala were themselves the only "tour guides" of their own destiny. Yes, Dalí may have ended his days like a vulnerable mortal, but he always demonstrated to have own an exceptional mind and affinity for the arts.

One thing is for sure, either because of that or something else, Dalí created a character in life, something like a living cartoon to suit his surreal personality. It certainly worked, he acted out based on his own unconscious dreams and believed in what he was doing, at least he was able to project the image of an inimitable "Artistic Madness to the Second Power." For the works he left behind, he truly deserves the title of " El Loco Divino." He definitely was someone people knew, hated or admired.

Most of us are glad that the admiration for him, it has happened that way. His paintings are found all over the civilized world. Since 1982 a wonderful "Dalí's Museum" exists in St. Petersburg, Fla., U.S. as well as in the town where he was born (Figueras, Spain.) The fully functioning "Salvador Dalí's" Museums speak proudly about the artist. His legacy lives on.

--- End ---

VULNERABLE EXCELLENCE

Salvador Dalí - A View to his life's Art & Legacy
by Emiliano Martín

Other (Poetry) chapbooks by Emiliano Martín:

511Aphorisms of my humor (2010)
Dream and Shadows (2002)
Moody Muse (2 001)
In the Company of Time (1999)
Whirlwind of Thoughts (1998)
Glazed by the Moon (1996)
In the Wilderness (1995)
Sparkles of Eternity (1994)
The Legacy of a Poet (1988)

CPSIA information can be obtained
at www.ICGtesting.com
Printed in the USA
BVHW070547130819
555662BV00009B/1282/P